Mystery at Loch Ness

Mystery at Loch Ness

BY ROY WANDELMAIER

Illustrated by Kim Mulkey

TROLL ASSOCIATES

Library of Congress Cataloging in Publication Data

Wandelmaier, Roy.
   Mystery at Loch Ness.

   Summary: While vacationing in Scotland, the reader
becomes involved in searching for a missing professor
who has been investigating the Loch Ness monster and
is provided with some fantastic choices to make.
    1. Plot-your-own stories. 2. Children's stories,
American. [1. Scotland—Fiction. 2. Fantasy.
3. Plot-your-own stories] I. Mulkey, Kim, ill.
II. Title.
PZ7.W179My   1985   [Fic]   85-2532
ISBN 0-8167-0529-1 (lib. bdg.)
ISBN 0-8167-0530-5 (pbk.)

We Hope You Enjoy
This Adventure Story

Just remember to read it differently than you would most other books. Start on page 1 and keep reading till you come to a choice. After that the story is up to you. Your decisions will take you from page to page.

Think carefully before you decide. Some choices will lead you to exciting, heroic, and happy endings. But watch out! Other choices can quickly lead to disaster.

Now you are ready to begin. The best of luck in your adventure!

Mystery at Loch Ness

You are spending the last four weeks of your summer vacation visiting your cousin Derek in Scotland. Together you have spent a lot of time hiking and camping in the Scottish highlands. It is a beautiful country, with its farms and fields, its sheep and Black Angus cattle.

One afternoon you are home watching television when you hear a news bulletin: A scientist, Professor Amanda Gregory, has been reported missing near Loch Ness. Her photograph flashes on the TV screen. She had been trying to find the Loch Ness monster—the legendary creature of Scotland's most famous lake—using the most up-to-date scientific equipment.

Professor Gregory is one of the leading authorities on prehistoric life. She believes that if the Loch Ness monster really exists, it may be a surviving member of an order of big, swimming reptiles thought to be extinct for millions of years.

Dr. Gregory's equipment was found untouched at her campsite. Her dinner was half-eaten and there was no sign of a struggle. She just seems to have walked away and vanished.

"Loch Ness is only four miles from here," says Derek, sipping his hot chocolate. "I bet we could find Dr. Gregory."

Turn to page 2.

from page 1

"Do you think there really is a Loch Ness monster?" you ask.

"Many people think there is," says Derek. "But I'm not so sure. We'll keep our eyes open, though."

You decide to take your bicycles and your camping equipment, and ride out to the famous lake immediately.

The ride takes you through beautiful forests and highland meadows. When you arrive at the lake, it is already late afternoon. You see search parties looking for Dr. Gregory along the shoreline. On the highest hill stand the ruins of an old castle.

"Everyone has already looked by the water," says Derek. "But I'll bet no one has looked up by the castle." You start hiking up to the castle. However, it begins to get dark sooner than you expected. Fog is forming on the lake below.

If you want to push on to the castle, turn to page 7.

If you want to camp where you are, in a grove of trees overlooking the lake, turn to page 4.

4

You camp in the grove overlooking the lake. After pitching your tent, you unroll your sleeping bags, eat a light dinner, and talk about your search plans for tomorrow. It does not take you long to fall asleep.

Something wakes you in the middle of the night. Derek is still asleep, but you peek out of the tent. What you see amazes you: a tiny man, about twelve inches tall, covered with hair and a long beard that stretches down to his feet.

Could this be one of the "little people" of Scottish folklore? You want to wake up Derek, but suddenly the little man walks away into the dark forest.

Turn to page 8.

You scan the room. Lying around are some old chairs, a wooden chest, and a thick carpet. An old tapestry of a unicorn hangs on the wall. A strong cord hangs from the ceiling.

"There must be a secret passage," says Derek. "It seems unusual that a tower room like this would have only one entrance."

You tap on the walls, but they are made of solid rock. You move the carpet and the chest, but nothing is underneath. You must find something fast. The iron door is strong, but the men are weakening it with their guns and axes. The only things you have not checked yet are the unicorn tapestry and the cord hanging from the ceiling.

If you want to look behind the tapestry, turn to page 22.

If you want to pull the cord, turn to page 31.

7

from page 2

You keep on walking up the hill to the castle. Soon the gathering fog reaches you, and you can't see far in front of you. But Derek knows the woods well. He says the castle is not far away. When you finally get to the castle, you see the old walls, many of which have fallen down over the centuries. One tower is still standing.

Now it is night.

"The fog is too thick to see the lake tonight," says Derek. All you can see are the lights of a small village on the far side of the lake.

You pitch your tent just inside the castle walls. Tomorrow you'll be able to look again for Dr. Gregory.

The world seems very different when you are in the woods at night. And tonight it is especially quiet, until you hear a soft moaning sound. You and Derek peek out of your sleeping bags. The sound seems to be coming from the castle tower.

If you want to climb the stone staircase up to the tower, turn to page 27.

If you want to leave the castle and pitch your tent in a grove of trees, turn to page 4.

from page 4

Leaving Derek asleep in the tent, you quietly follow the tiny man through the woods. Soon you come to a meadow. Here, beneath the full moon, are many other little people and fairies. They are dancing and playing strange music. Around and around the fairies dance. Fireflies blink.

If you want to walk into this meadow, turn to page 13.

If you want to remain hidden, turn to page 16.

You go out and say hello to the three men. Perhaps they are fellow searchers, looking for Dr. Gregory. They are certainly surprised to see you. "What are you doing here?" snarls one. They pull out guns from their pockets.

Just then you hear a howl again, just outside the castle walls. A silver wolf bounds out of the forest. The three men turn in fear and shoot at the wolf.

If you want to run into the tower and lock the door, turn to page 11.

If you want to do nothing, turn to page 14.

10

You try to remember what you have heard about fairies. Don't they kidnap young people? You are on your guard.

"Normally we would never allow a mortal to see us," she says. "But I know why you have come. You need our help tonight, and we may be able to use yours.

"Know this: there is much evil that has come to the forest. And the woman you seek is in trouble. If you act quickly, you can save her. You may find her at *Farnost*." She touches you gently on the forehead.

Before you can ask what she means, Titania and her fairies vanish. The firefly lights go out, and you are left alone in the meadow. All that remains is a large circle of mushrooms.

From where you stand, you now have a clear view of the lake. In the moonlight, you think you can see a dark object on the water. Is it an animal or a boat?

If you want to go down to the lake, turn to page 29.

If you want to go back to your tent to talk to Derek, turn to page 15.

You enter the room, close the door, and bolt it shut. Soon you hear a pounding on the door, shouting, then gunfire. You know you're going to have to find another way out of this room. Quickly you and Derek try to find an escape route.

Turn to page 5.

from page 8

You enter the fairy ring, hoping they will not all run away. But they keep on dancing and singing. A beautiful woman speaks to you: "Welcome," she says. "I am Titania, queen of the night spirits. We were hoping you would come."

Turn to page 10.

14

from page 9

The men shoot wildly and miss the wolf. But the shots scare the animal. It runs back into the depths of the forest. You breathe a sigh of relief.

Unfortunately, the men now turn their guns on you and Derek. You are never heard from again.

THE END

You hike back to your tent. But when you get there, Derek is gone. You call for him, though you don't want to call out too loudly. Derek's sleeping bag is still warm. First Dr. Gregory seems to have walked away. Now Derek. The only place you have not been tonight is the castle. You reluctantly decide to go there.

Turn to page 85.

from page 8

You decide to remain hidden. It is wonderful just to watch the magical dance. Their beautiful music begins to relax you. Before you know it, you fall sound asleep.

When you wake up, it is still night. All is quiet. The fairies are gone. But you notice something strange right away. The entire forest seems to have grown enormously. Mushrooms are now as tall as you are. Stones and bushes tower over your head.

Then you understand: the forest is still the same size. You must have shrunk. You are now about four inches tall!

Something else about you has changed. You can see, hear, smell, and feel more clearly than ever before.

A mouse scurries along. "Don't stand there," she says. "The owl is out tonight. You can come with me if you like."

If you want to run back to your tent, turn to page 18.

If you want to run with the mouse, turn to page 20.

18

You would rather go back to your tent. You want to talk to Derek. Maybe he can figure out a way to help you. You walk back carefully, on the alert for a hungry owl. You don't want to be anyone's dinner.

When you get to the tent, you see it is empty. Derek's sleeping bag is still warm, but he is gone.

A small bird lands near you and says, "I saw men take your friend down to the lake. I will take you there, if you would like to go."

You must help Derek, so you hop on the bird's back and ride down to the lake. There you see three men loading Derek onto a boat, against his will. They put Derek in the small cabin, and the boat pulls quickly away from shore. With you still on its back, the bird flies after the boat.

No one notices you. The men are too busy watching the lake. Soon the boat nears the opposite shore. Beneath a big rock, a hidden wall begins to open.

Turn to page 21.

You decide it might be nice to stay this size. You would never have to go to school again. As the days pass, you learn how to survive in the wild and how to find food. Your friends are now the animals of the forest.

THE END

20

You run with the mouse through the forest. When a hawk flies overhead, the mouse stops to hide in a hollow log. You do the same. Everything looks different when you are this small. When danger is past, you run on.

Soon you arrive at the mouse's house: a tunnel under a fallen tree. Inside, the nest is covered with straw and dry grass. "You are welcome to what food I have," says the mouse.

You tell the mouse how you came to the forest in search of the missing scientist, Professor Amanda Gregory. You can't explain how you got to be so small.

"I do not know about any missing human," says the mouse. " But I am on my way to a council meeting at the Big Oak. If you would like to come along, we might ask the others."

You follow the mouse to the Big Oak.

Turn to page 34.

from page 18 / from page 33

The boat begins to slip through the opening into an underground tunnel.

If you want to drop down onto the boat in secret, turn to page 43.

If you want to remain outside on the big rock, turn to page 41.

22

You peek behind the unicorn tapestry. There is a wooden doorway! You both slip in and lock this door behind you. Shining your flashlights ahead of you, you walk down a narrow staircase inside the tower. Could Dr. Gregory have come this way?

Suddenly you come to a fork in the path. The left path continues going down. The right levels out and goes straight ahead.

If you want to keep going down, turn to page 36.

If you want to go straight, turn to page 38.

from page 34

"I'm sorry," you say, "but I must find Dr. Gregory. Have any of you seen her?"

"I saw her," says Raccoon. "Men took her to the other side of the lake, by the big rock."

"Can any of you show me how to get to the big rock?"

No animals volunteer except one: Skunk. "I'll take you," he says.

Go to page 25.

from page 24

The skunk lets you ride on his back. You are glad for the lift, because it is a long way to the big rock. The skunk moves quickly along the forest floor.

You trot through deep forest, then through fields and meadows. Suddenly, a huge wolf appears in front of you. It looks like the wolf wants to eat both of you for dinner. Your urge is to run, but the skunk stands his ground.

If you want to run for a nearby rabbit hole, turn to page 30.

If you want to stand with the skunk, turn to page 33.

from page 29

"Hello," you say to the fisherman.

"Hello, stranger," he says. "What brings you out on such a beautiful foggy night?"

"I'm camping with a friend up the hill," you tell him.

"I see you've met the fairies," says the man.

"How did you know that?"

"You still have the mark on your forehead." You touch your head, but feel nothing different.

"Do you know anything about fairies?" you ask.

"A few things. But I know more about fishing. I think I've got a nibble now." He pulls in his line and lifts something out of the water.

Turn to page 42.

Up the stone stairs you go, flashlights in hand. When you get to the top of the stairs, you see something that not even Derek has ever noticed: part of the stone wall of the tower has been broken away, revealing a slightly open iron door. The moaning is caused by the wind passing through the opening.

You shine your flashlights inside the room. Suddenly you notice three men coming up the hill toward the castle. Turning off your lights, you wonder what you should do. You hear a strange howl several hundred yards in another direction. Now you see the men are carrying shovels and pickaxes. They are climbing up the stairs to the tower.

If you want to meet these men, turn to page 9.

If you want to go inside the tower room and bolt the door shut, turn to page 11.

from page 10

Walking down to the lake, you notice that a wonderful change has come over you since meeting Titania. You can see much better in the dark. You can smell better, hear better. You feel both relaxed and excited in the night world.

When you reach the shore of the lake, however, you can no longer see any object on the water. No boat, no animal. Instead, you see a man sitting on a rock, fishing. His pants are a bit too large for him. He has a neat, white beard.

He doesn't seem to notice you.

If you want to talk to this man, turn to page 26.

If you want to hike back up the hill to your tent, turn to page 15.

from page 25

You run to the rabbit hole, and the wolf is pleased. Now it does not have to deal with the skunk. In a flash, the wolf is upon you.

THE END

You pull the cord. The shooting and banging outside the door stop. Instead you hear the sound of ancient gears moving, and cries of help from the men. For a long time all is quiet. Then you brave a look outside. The stairway has dropped down, sinking the three men in a pit with iron bars across the top.

"It must be the way the king defended this tower," says Derek. You are safe, for now.

"You think you're clever, don't you?" says one of the men. "Just wait until Mr. Shaw arrives. He'll free us and then you'll be sorry!"

If you want to go down the hill to try to find the police, turn to page 37.

If you want to go back in the room and look behind the unicorn tapestry, turn to page 22.

The men are either not careful or not lucky enough. The boat hits something in the water and begins to sink. The men can only try to swim back to shore.

Some kind of large water animal peeks its head above the water, then swims below. The men swim to shore, but the water is ice cold. You help fish them out of the water, and they surrender to you. They are wet, tired, and freezing. And they are scared to death of the king. Suddenly the police arrive! (You will always wonder how they found out you needed help.)

The men lead you to their hide-out. There you find Dr. Gregory safe. You and Derek are heroes, and King Malcolm is free at last. Now that you are friends, the king promises to visit you at your home next summer.

THE END

from page 25

___

You stand your ground with the skunk. Fortunately, the wolf does not want to attack the skunk. The wolf slinks away.

Now that you are safe, you proceed with your journey. At last you reach the big rock, which hangs out over the lake. You thank Skunk, and he goes back to his forest. Now you are alone. When you look out at the lake, you are just in time to see a boat sailing toward you. With your keen eyesight, you pick out three men on board. They are holding a fourth person prisoner—it is Derek!

Below you, a wall of rock begins to open. It is a secret entrance.

___

Turn to page 21.

from page 20

Beneath the Big Oak, you meet Rabbit, Raccoon, Cricket, Skunk, Hedgehog, Toad, and Squirrel. Mouse introduces you to everyone, and you tell them about your search.

"Forget about this other human," suggests Toad. "Be thankful for your good fortune—you are now a wonderful size. Why would you want to deal with humans anymore? Stay with us here in the forest."

If you want to stay in the forest with the animals, turn to page 19.

If you want to keep searching for Dr. Gregory, turn to page 24.

36

You keep walking down, but the tunnel never seems to end. Finally you hear the sound of dripping water.

Turn to page 44.

from page 31

You make your way down the hill as quickly as possible in the dark. Then you hike along the shore until you come to the nearest village. By the time you can get police officers to come up to the castle, it is morning. The men are gone, and the tower has been destroyed by explosives. Not a clue remains. Dr. Gregory is never heard from again.

THE END

38

You keep walking and enter an underground room. You and Derek may be the first two people to enter this room since it was built centuries ago. In the middle of the room stands a wooden box. On the other side of the room is a wooden door.

If you want to open the box, turn to page 51.

If you want to open the door, turn to page 53.

Moving aside the barrels, you find a trap door! You open the door and follow a long tunnel down into the earth.

Turn to page 36.

from page 21

You are cautious, and you do not just want to walk into such an unknown place. You would like to think about it for a little while.

Just then a large hand grabs you and picks you up. The hand belongs to an old woman, who puts you carefully into a burlap sack. The sack is full of fresh mushrooms and herbs.

After a long walk in the dark, you are pulled out of the sack and put into a small cage on a wooden table.

The woman is stirring soup in a black kettle. "Toil and trouble from morning till night," she says, "but you will certainly taste good in my soup."

Turn to page 50.

from page 26

The fisherman reels in an old shoe. Far away you hear a dog howling at the full moon.

"These are not easy times for fairies," he says.

Then you see the thing on the water again. But this time you can clearly see that it is a boat.

"See that boat?" you whisper. "I think that's what I saw before. I thought it was the Loch Ness monster."

"You'll know Nessie when you see her," says the man. "I've been watching that boat, too. Been watching it for the last two weeks. It only comes out after dark, and I can tell you this: they're not out fishing."

Then a searchlight flashes on and off. The light seems to be aimed at you.

"Come on," says the fisherman. "We can hide behind these rocks." The fisherman scampers back among the bigger rocks, but slips and falls.

If you want to help the fisherman, turn to page 49.

If you want to do nothing, turn to page 54.

from page 21

You drop down onto the boat behind the cabin. No one notices you as the boat motors underground. As the rock wall closes behind you, you strain to see ahead in the darkness. Then a bright light appears in front of you. You have entered a great underground lake . . . a lake under the mountain.

Turn to page 46.

44

You walk until the tunnel opens up into a large cavern with a lake in the middle. With your flashlights, you can see an old boat rotting on the shore of the underground lake. "Perhaps the king of the castle used this tunnel as an escape route," says Derek.

Suddenly you hear a noise and see a light at the other end of the lake. So this is not a dead end. You quickly turn off your lights and hide behind some rocks. You hear men's voices. A small rowboat is coming toward you.

"I tell you I thought I saw a light and heard voices back here. We've never come back this far—this place is just too creepy for me. Who knows where all these streams come from?"

They sweep their own flashlights around the cavern. They stop when they see the old boat, but don't seem to care about it. You are too well hidden to be seen.

Go to page 45.

"Probably one of those cavefish made the noise," says the other man. "Or maybe you're starting to hear things. Let's go back."

After they row away, you follow their light along the side of the lake. They lead you to a well-lit underground room, even bigger than the first one. There are more men here, as well as supplies, guns, shovels, and a tent. There is also Dr. Amanda Gregory! And it looks like she is being held captive. You have found some kind of hide-out, and these men are clearly up to no good.

"All right, let's go," says one of the men. "It's time to meet Mr. Shaw up at the site. Let's leave the professor here. She looks a little too tied-up to go anywhere herself."

The man turns a pulley. Where there was once just a rock wall, a doorway now opens out onto a large body of water—Loch Ness itself.

Turn to page 89.

from page 43

The men take Derek off the boat and bring him to a small camping area. There are tents here, with cots, food, supplies, ammunition, and another prisoner: Dr. Amanda Gregory!

Derek is brought into the tent and handcuffed next to Dr. Gregory. The men don't say much. All you can do is wait until you can think of something to do.

An hour goes by, then another. Finally all of the men but one get in the boat. They are leaving.

"We'll meet Mr. Shaw up at the site," says one of the men. "Then we'll bring down the treasure. It should just take another hour to get it out of the room. Then we'll be back to get you," he says to the remaining man.

"Well, hurry," says the man who is staying. "This place gives me the creeps."

After the men leave, the lone guard sits down outside the tent and reads a magazine.

Turn to page 75.

"I know this looks bad," you try to cheer up Derek, "but someone may find us in a few days."

"Harrumph!"

That was not Derek's voice. Out of the darkness, you see a shimmering white light. There is someone else in the room—a ghost! As the light gets a bit stronger, you can see the ghost's face—he looks just like the painting of the ancient king, Malcolm Gregory.

Turn to page 77.

You help the fisherman hide behind a rock. The searchlight passes over you, then goes out. The boat waits a minute longer, then speeds away across the lake, out of sight.

"That was a close one," says the fisherman. "Thank you. My name is Angus Stewart. I see Titania chose you wisely."

Turn to page 55.

from page 41

"You can't eat me!" you say, "I'm a human being, just like you."

"Eat you I will, but not right away," she says. "This broth must cook overnight. Good night, until tomorrow."

The old woman goes into the next room. Soon she is snoring peacefully. But sleep is the last thing on your mind.

In a few moments, you see a little man enter the room. The little man does not notice you. He is cleaning the old woman's kitchen, washing her dishes, and mending her socks.

"Psst," you whisper. "Will you help me please? Will you free me?"

The little man frees you at once, and you thank him. But as you start to leave, the man silently motions for you to come back. He points to a kitchen cabinet beneath the sink. He seems to want you to open the cabinet.

If you want to open the cabinet, turn to page 61.

If you want to get out of the house, turn to page 57.

Together you are able to lift the heavy wooden lid of the chest. Inside is treasure: gold and silver, Roman coins and jewelry.

Then you are startled by a sharp voice: "Stop. Don't move an inch."

You turn to see a gang of men standing at the doorway.

"That is our treasure," says a man. You try to explain that you are just campers.

"Too bad," he says. "We can't allow you to leave. We're going to have to get rid of you, but you can have a choice. Would you rather be locked in the room behind that door? Or would you prefer to be taken out to the middle of the Loch and thrown over the side of our boat?"

Decisions like these you wish you did not have to make.

If you would rather be locked in the storage room, turn to page 83.

If you would rather be pushed overboard into the Loch, turn to page 80.

from page 38

With your flashlights on, you open the door and walk into a small room. All kinds of curious objects lie around: pieces of armor, old barrels, a portrait of a king on the wall. But the room seems to be a dead end.

Suddenly the door slams behind you. You run over to the door, then pause. Did someone push the door shut? You try to listen, but there is no sound from the outside room. Maybe you should not go through that door right away. Could there be another way out?

You try to find a secret passage, but there are no hollow places in the wall. Neither of you wants to give up yet. There are still these curious objects in the room.

If you want to look behind the portrait, turn to page 90.

If you want to move aside the barrels, turn to page 39.

54

from page 42

Spotting you in its searchlight, the boat speeds over to you. The fisherman disappears into the woods. The boat stops about thirty yards from the shore, with its lights off.

"Mr. Shaw?" asks one of the men on the boat.

"That's not him," says another voice on the boat. "Let's get out of here!" The boat speeds away across the lake. You are left alone. Now all you can do is return to your tent.

When you get to the tent, Derek is gone. A wolf is howling, and you are alone in the woods. The wolf is getting closer . . . .

THE END

from page 49

You are not sure what he means, but you like Angus Stewart. You tell him how you and your friend Derek have come looking for Dr. Amanda Gregory. Then you tell him how you met Titania, queen of the night spirits, and what she told you. "'You may find her at Farnost,' Titania said, but I don't know what that means."

"Farnost. That was the fairies' name for the castle on the hill."

"Will you help me find her?" you ask.

"All right," says Angus. "But did you say you had a friend camping up near there?"

"Yes. Is there anything the matter?"

The fisherman won't say anything except, "We'd better find him."

When you and Angus reach the tent, Derek is gone!

You hear the howling of a wolf about a hundred yards away. The animal is moving toward you.

"Trouble," says Angus.

If you want to take some food and climb a tree, turn to page 59.

If you want to protect yourselves by lighting a fire, turn to page 60.

from page 87

You stand your ground. The men pull out guns and start shooting at you!

By luck, the first few bullets miss you and Angus. You both turn and run down the hill. Somehow you get separated in the dark. You run through the woods, tripping over rocks and sliding on leaves.

Soon you are lost in the forest. You wonder if you will ever be able to find Angus, or Derek, again.

THE END

from page 50

You want to leave the woman's house immediately. You dash out the front door, down a path and onto an old dirt road. You can still see the Loch in front of you, so you hope you can retrace your steps back to the secret entrance again.

By now your small size is no longer a bad thing. You won't get caught napping again, either. You find the secret entrance by the big rock. But there is no way for you to get inside.

If you want to wait by the entrance, turn to page 64.

If you want to walk back to your tent, turn to page 62.

from page 55

You and Angus climb the nearest tree, carrying the rest of the food from your tent. You have the instant cocoa. Angus has Derek's leftover hamburgers. Just in time you reach the first branches. A werewolf leaps into the clearing and dashes into your tent, rummaging through your belongings. Sniffing in the air, he spots you climbing the tree.

The werewolf runs to your tree. "Throw him the hamburgers," you tell Angus, hoping they will satisfy the werewolf. Angus tosses the burgers. The werewolf gobbles them down in a minute. Unfortunately, they only seem to whet his appetite for the two of you.

Turn to page 87.

from page 55

You quickly try to light a fire, but it is too late. You throw rocks at the wolf as it leaps at you. The end is too horrible to tell.

THE END

You open the cabinet and look inside. The cabinet is full of old rags, but also bottles of liquids. The bottles are all carefully labeled: *Hair strengthener. Fat remover. Size restorer!* There is also a tin can full of gold coins.

First you drink the size restorer. It works! You are easily changed back to your normal size.

Now you have to make another decision. What do you want to do about the gold? The old woman is still snoring.

If you want to take the gold, turn to page 72.

If you want to leave without the gold, turn to page 78.

62

You begin the long walk back along the shore. Soon morning breaks and something nice happens. Maybe it is the sun, or maybe the spell is just wearing off, but you are changing back to your former size. Soon you are normal again. And you find new strength.

Turn to page 95.

from page 87

You and Angus run down the hill as fast as you can. Fireflies guide you safely. The men behind you, on the other hand, are having a difficult time. Tree roots trip them, and cobwebs get in their eyes. They shoot their guns wildly and soon run out of bullets. A huge silver wolf chases two of the men up a tree.

When you reach the lake, a police boat is waiting. The criminals run right into their trap. After the men surrender, they lead you to their hide-out. There you find Derek and Dr. Amanda Gregory, who have been held prisoner. They are safe, and happy to see you.

The best surprise of all: you find the buried treasure of old King Malcolm beneath the walls of the castle. That is what the men were looking for.

Turn to page 71.

64

Fifteen minutes go by, then half an hour. Dawn is not far away. After an hour has gone by, you hear the muffled sound of a boat engine. The rock wall is opening!

The boat comes out, this time with four men aboard, but no Derek. After the boat moves onto the lake, the door begins to shut. This may be your only chance. You sneak inside just as the rock door closes behind you. Luckily there is a bright light inside. You have entered a big underground cavern.

It is a hide-out, stocked with tents, supplies, and guns. A man is sitting outside the tents reading a magazine. Being so small, you can easily creep about unnoticed. Peeking in the back of the main tent, you find Derek and a woman—it can only be Dr. Amanda Gregory—handcuffed inside. You've found them.

Turn to page 75.

from page 80

You are too cold to be frightened. Nessie swims under you, then gently rises. With both of you on its back, the lake creature swims quickly to the village on the far shore. Then Nessie deposits you on dry land. A fisherman finds you and unties you. You are able to call the police and catch the criminals just before they escape. The police recover the treasure and also find Dr. Gregory, who was held captive in an underground hide-out.

The Loch Ness monster is nowhere to be seen. You and Derek get your pictures in the newspaper, and the treasure is given to the university museum. All the reporters want to know how you escaped. But you and Derek have agreed that it will remain your secret— and Nessie's.

THE END

from page 89

Up the tunnel you climb, until you come to a fork. One path keeps going up. You take the other, which goes straight ahead and leads you to an underground room. In the middle of the room is a big wooden box.

"Could that be the treasure?" asks Dr. Gregory.

The three of you lift the heavy lid. Inside is a magnificent sight: gold and silver, Roman coins and jewelry. It looks like you have found King Malcolm's treasure first. But you know the crooks will be here soon. What are you going to do?

There is a door at the other end of this room. You open it. A short tunnel leads you up a short flight of stairs and out into the castle courtyard. Dawn is not far away. You hear a moan. Then you see something up on the tower of the castle. It is a ghost, and he has seen you.

If you want to confront the ghost, turn to page 74.

If you want to go back downstairs to the treasure room, turn to page 91.

from page 80

Frightened to death of this monster, you try to get away from it. The lake creature disappears beneath the surface and is gone.

You don't last a minute in the freezing water.

THE END

You pull the lever and raise the secret door. The three of you step outside. But then your hearts sink. Standing there staring at you is a man. But he does not look like the other men. He is older, has a white beard, and his pants look too short.

Turn to page 73.

from page 63

Later you thank Angus for his help. You wonder out loud how the police knew where to be at just the right moment.

"Maybe we have Titania to thank for that," says Angus. He is looking up the hill at the lights of the fireflies.

You and Derek are glad to have had this adventure, but you hope the rest of your vacation will be more peaceful. "I know just where I want to go camping next weekend," you tell Derek. You tell him about the beautiful meadow—but not about the fairies —on your way home.

THE END

from page 61

You take the gold, but this wakes up the old woman. She is so angry that she turns you into a newt. Now she wants to cook you immediately. Luckily you manage to escape.

You scurry out into the woods, to spend the rest of your life as an amphibian.

THE END

from page 69

Professor Gregory speaks to him. "Are you Mr. Shaw?"

"No. My name is Stewart. Angus Stewart."

"Can you help us, Mr. Stewart?" asks Derek.

"It depends," says Mr. Stewart. "Whose side are you on?"

"I'm not sure," you say. "There is a gang of treasure thieves, and they're on their way up to the castle. They're going to try to steal King Malcolm's treasure. We've got to stop them. We've got to call the police before the thieves get away."

"Listen," says Mr. Stewart. "Come with me. There's no time to get the police right now."

If you want to go find the police, turn to page 94.

If you want to go with Angus Stewart, turn to page 79.

74

from page 67

You decide to face the ghost as bravely as you can. He slowly floats down and stands before the three of you.

"My name is Malcolm," says the ghost, looking at you with suspicion. "I was once the king of this castle."

You politely introduce yourselves. "We didn't mean to trespass," you explain, "but there are evil men on the way here. They intend to steal your treasure, and we want to stop them if we can."

"If I were you, I would let them have it," says King Malcolm. "That treasure has done me not one bit of good all these years. In fact, there is a curse on it. I wish someone would take it away. Then the curse would be lifted.

"On the other hand," says the king, "I wouldn't want *thieves* to have my treasure. What am I going to do?"

Turn to page 93.

Suddenly you spot a key hitched to the tent. Perhaps you can unlock the handcuffs. But how are you going to distract the guard? And then how are you going to figure out how to get out of the hide-out? You see two pulleys. You hope one operates the secret door.

You throw a pebble into the lake, behind the guard. He looks up, then goes back to his magazine. You throw another pebble farther upstream. The guard picks up his gun and goes to check on the noise.

Then, not knowing which pulley does what, you crank both. The secret door begins to open!

You quickly shut off the kerosene lamp. The cave is now pitch dark. But enough dawn light enters the cave for your extra-sharp eyesight. The guard yells, but he can't see a thing.

You take the key to Derek and Dr. Gregory. They free themselves. "I'll explain later, Derek. Just follow me," you say.

Turn to page 98.

from page 48

"Imagine," says the ghost. "Those men are stealing my treasure, after all these years."

"We can stop them, your majesty," says Derek, "if you can help us get out of here."

"I don't want to stop them," says the ghost. "Let them have it all and much good may it do them. That treasure cursed me. Now I am free. I don't have to stay here in this cold collection of rocks anymore. Now I can go anywhere I please."

"May we have your help anyway?" you ask.

"I'm sorry, but I cannot help you."

"Your majesty, those men are not just treasure thieves. We believe they have kidnapped a famous scientist."

"What is a 'scientist'?" asks the king.

You try to explain. "She came here to study the Loch Ness monster. Her name is Dr. Amanda Gregory."

"Gregory? Did you say Gregory? My name is also Gregory. Those men have captured a Gregory! You'll find a key to the door in this barrel. Hurry."

Turn to page 82.

from page 61

You don't want to risk taking gold which does not belong to you. And you don't want to spend another minute in the old woman's house. You dash out the front door, down a path, and onto a dirt road. You are free, but lost. Do you think you can ever find the secret cave? You hope Derek is all right. You are willing to bet that the same men who took Derek also took Dr. Gregory.

It is now late at night. You walk back toward the lake, and search for the secret entrance. But you can't find the big rock anymore. Your keen eyesight seems to have gone with your small size.

All you can do is walk back to your tent and then find the police. As dawn breaks, you can see the old castle on the hill.

Turn to page 95.

from page 73

"O.K., Mr. Stewart. We're with you. Let's try our best."

"Excellent, but please call me Angus," he says. "And we don't have to do that much. I've already sent word up to the castle."

"How did you do that?" asks Dr. Gregory. "Sent word to whom?"

But Angus does not answer. He leads you quickly up the hill.

Turn to page 96.

80

from page 51

You figure you can always swim to shore, so you choose the boat. The men take you and Derek down to their boat, then out to the middle of the lake.

"There's only one thing we forgot to mention," says the leader. "We'll have to tie your hands and feet. We wouldn't want you to just swim away."

As soon as you are tied, the men push you overboard. The boat speeds away.

It will be the perfect crime. The men will take away the treasure, and there will be no witnesses. You can probably stay afloat for only a few more seconds. The cold water pierces through you.

Then something unexpected happens. A big head rises out of the water near you. It is the Loch Ness monster!

If you want to get away from the monster, turn to page 68.

If you want to go to the monster, turn to page 66.

from page 77

With King Malcolm in the lead, you escape from the underground rooms. Just in time, you spot the men carrying the treasure chest down the hill to their boat.

If you want to run down the hill after the men, turn to page 84.

If you want to start a signal fire to alert the police, turn to page 86.

from page 51

You choose the storage room. The men search it quickly, to make sure there is no door or secret passage you can use to escape.

Finding nothing, they take away your flashlights and lock you inside—in total darkness. All you remember seeing before they closed the door are some old pieces of armor, barrels, and an old portrait hanging on the wall.

"A portrait of the old king, Malcolm Gregory," whispers Derek. "He built this castle in the thirteenth century." You try to find a secret passage, too. You quietly tap against walls, ceiling, and floor. You move aside the barrels and look behind the portrait. Nothing. Now it is silent outside your room. The men must have left with the treasure. You may be in this room a long time.

Turn to page 48.

84

King Malcolm leads you out of the castle and down the hill. But what can you do? The criminals have guns. You have nothing. Then something strange begins to happen. Branches reach out to brush the faces of the men. Cobwebs get in their eyes. King Malcolm flies up in the air, moaning. That makes the men run even faster. In a panic, they finally reach their boat and hurl the treasure chest on board.

They race their boat away from the shore. It looks as if you'll never be able to stop them now.

Turn to page 32.

from page 15

The castle is just where you find Derek. He came up here to look for you.

Suddenly you both hear a noise. Someone or something is walking in the woods toward you. Remembering Titania's warning about evil in the forest, you ask Derek to hide with you. He does not need to be persuaded. But where are you going to hide? A section of the castle wall has recently fallen down. Behind the wall, you see what may be an entrance to an underground tunnel. Then you hear another noise—a quiet moaning. It is coming from the tower.

If you want to hide in the tunnel, turn to page 38.

If you want to hide in the tower, turn to page 27.

from page 82

The king helps you start a bright fire on the top of the castle tower. And soon the police arrive. But it is too late to stop the criminals from getting away with the treasure.

THE END

Just then you hear strange music coming from the woods, music like you heard at the fairies' dance. The werewolf trots away peacefully back into the forest. You don't think you'll have any more trouble from it for a while.

"I sure hope Derek didn't meet that werewolf," you say.

"Not if he is as quick-thinking as you," says Angus. "I think we had better look up at the castle for him."

Not much is left of the castle. Walls have fallen down over the centuries, and only one tower remains standing.

Then you hear the sound of shovels digging against rock. Angus whispers, "No one is supposed to be digging here—especially at night."

You creep over to look around one of the crumbled walls. You see five men, digging a deep hole in the ground. Guns lie nearby.

"Should be only a few more feet," says one of them. "Then we'll have the treasure. By tomorrow we'll be rich men."

Unfortunately, one of the men spots you. "Hey!" he yells.

If you want to run away down the hill, turn to page 63.

If you want to do nothing, turn to page 56.

After the men leave, you free Dr. Gregory. She is surprised and delighted to meet the two of you. She explains: "Those men are treasure thieves. They believe the stories of the lost treasure of King Malcolm. And they have been digging at night up at the castle for the last several weeks. I only discovered this two days ago. I got too close, and they brought me down here to keep me quiet.

"Tonight they're meeting their boss, Mr. Shaw, up at the castle. He's the one who paid for all this.

"We've got to stop them. That treasure belongs to all the citizens of Scotland, not to these thieves. We should go out the secret door to alert the police."

Derek does not agree. "That will take too long. The crooks would get away. It will be faster to go back up the tunnel to the castle. Then we could see what they do." Your vote is needed to make the decision.

If you want to go back up the tunnel, turn to page 67.

If you want to go out the secret door, turn to page 69.

from page 53

You move aside the portrait, but there is nothing behind it. Then you look at the back of the painting. All you see are the letters of some old language. This leads you nowhere.

If you want to check the barrels, turn to page 39.

If you want to leave this room and look inside the wooden chest in the next room, turn to page 51.

from page 67

Treasure thieves are one thing, but you don't want to tangle with a ghost. You run back down the tunnel to the treasure room and close the door behind you. But the door closes with a loud thud. You can't open it, nor can you open the trap door which would take you back to the underground cavern. You are trapped.

THE END

from page 74

Before you can decide what to do, the men appear outside the walls of the castle. They have guns and shovels, and there is nothing you can do to stop them.

From a hiding place, you watch helplessly as the thieves take the treasure from the underground room. They carry it down the hill, and you follow them in secret, hoping for a chance to stop them. But you can do nothing.

The men load the treasure chest onto their waiting boat, then speed away across the lake, a clean getaway.

But as they sail across the lake, something goes wrong. The boat hits something in the water and begins to sink.

Turn to page 99.

from page 73

You thank Mr. Stewart, but you really think this is a matter for the police. The police may be miles away. You start a big signal fire, and it works. The police arrive in less than an hour.

But by the time you make your way up to the castle, it is too late. You find an underground room which no one knew was ever there. Inside stands an empty wooden chest. Was there a treasure inside? You may never know . . .

THE END

from page 62 / from page 78

When you finally reach the campsite, you get a wonderful surprise. Derek is there, and so is Dr. Amanda Gregory! Down at the shore, police are escorting six criminals onto a waiting police boat. Derek can't wait to tell you what an adventure he just had. You can't wait to tell him about yours.

THE END

from page 79

When you arrive, you find the crooks sound asleep within the walls of the castle. They don't look like they will wake up for a while.

"Thanks to the fairies, we can now signal the police," says Angus. "And we should even find a treasure below that hole." You can see a deep pit where the men had been digging.

You and Derek and Angus and Dr. Gregory continue digging as you wait for the police. Before long, you hit an iron door in the earth. You uncover the door, open it, and discover an underground room. Inside is a great wooden chest full of gold and silver. You have solved the mystery!

When you turn around to thank Angus, he is gone.

The police finally arrive to take the criminals to jail. Dr. Gregory arranges to have the treasure taken to the university and tells you that you will receive a reward! You and Derek pack up your camping equipment and ride your bicycles home. You are ready for a well-deserved cup of hot chocolate and a good night's sleep.

THE END

98

from page 75

The three of you jump into a spare boat and speed away through the secret door. Out on the Loch, something wonderful happens. Maybe it is the morning sun or maybe the spell is wearing off, but you return to your normal size before the astonished eyes of your two companions.

You speed to the nearest village and find the police. They capture the men and a chest full of treasure, just before the crooks can make their getaway.

You and Derek and Dr. Gregory share the reward for the capture. You are heroes.

THE END

"That's impossible," says Derek. "Loch Ness is hundreds of feet deep." In the dawn light, you think you see some kind of animal stick its head above the water, then dive below. The men can do nothing to save the sinking treasure. They only want to get themselves out of the ice-cold water. The sinking boat has alerted an early-morning search party, and the police are called. The thieves are all captured when they reach shore.

You have rescued Dr. Gregory, and the curse of King Malcolm's treasure has now been lifted. You can almost hear the trees and hills breathe a sigh of relief. The grateful ghost is now free to leave the castle. You say good-bye to him and to your new friend, Dr. Gregory.

As you and Derek ride your bicycles home, you can't resist asking him, "Care to go camping tomorrow night?"

"I think I would prefer some hot chocolate, and a nice warm chair in front of the fireplace," says Derek.

You think that is a splendid idea.

THE END